From an Acorn to an Oak
The Story of Rooty Eike

Shine

Angela Q. Bertone

2018

Edited by Emily Mayeaux

Book cover design by Ariane O'Pry Trammell

Illustrated by Ariane O'Pry Trammell

ISBN-13:978-1501073946

ISBN-10:150107394X

Library of Congress cataloging registered

Bertone, Angela Q.

Rooty Eike

DEDICATION

I dedicate this book to my husband, Michael. He is my inspiration for this work. As we travel across America working to help people recover from storms, he takes every opportunity to find and bring home acorns of all types.

With great care he nurtures each one from an acorn to an oak. While watching him plant these wonderful trees with our first grandchild, the story of Rooty was born. I would make up bits and pieces and try them out with Anna at bedtime, and the wonder in her eyes inspired me more and more. The story you are about to read has captivated the heart of my granddaughter and my husband, and I hope it captivates yours as well.

Thank you, Michael, for being you, and allowing me the honor to show a part of your character to the world. I love you.

ACKNOWLEDGMENTS

With a grateful heart I say thank you to Michael Bertone, Sr. You are my best friend, a wonderful father and the husband I prayed for.

You believe in me when I can't believe in myself, encourage me when I put my dreams on the shelf, challenge me when my work is not the best it can be and rejoice with me in seeing my dreams come true.

Thank you, honey, for all that you have done and all that you do to encourage and support me.

Words can't express what I feel in my heart for you, so I will spend my life showing you.

Once upon a time there was an old man called Paw Paw. Paw Paw loved his grandchildren, and he loved the forest too. One of his favorite things to do was to sit in a big swing that hung in his favorite oak tree. It was there that he told the most wonderful stories to all of his grandchildren.

One day while swinging in the cool breeze with all of his grandchildren gathered around him, he told the story of Rooty Eike.

"Once upon a time," said PawPaw, "in this majestic forest, stood the grandest of trees where an amazing little acorn named Rooty lived. He was the happiest little acorn you ever did see. He loved hanging on his mother's branch and would sing with the rain, *drip-drop . . . drip-drop*. He would dance with the wind, swinging *swish-swish, swish-swish* back and forth.

One hot and muggy day, everything changed when a big, mean storm came with great destruction in its winds and blew right into my forest.

The air was filled with sadness. The little acorn cried when he saw all the trees falling; he tried with all his might to hang on to the branch of his mother. *Crack, creak, pop* went the branch as the wind blew. 'Help me, Mother, help!" he screamed, but the wind was too strong for his mother to hold on and her branch broke. The little acorn fell down, down, down with a great big *thud*. The ground was hard, wet and lonely.

"After the storm moved on, the little acorn cried again, 'Help me, Mother, help!' but there was nothing his mother could do. She could not put the little acorn back. Her branch was broken. She tried to comfort the little acorn by telling him to be courageous, and that in time he would grow to be a grand oak tree just like her. 'We will live together in this forest side by side.

Be patient, little one,' she said. 'For there will come a season when you will not see me and you will feel all alone. But have faith and believe, because everything that you need is inside of you. Never lose hope, and when you are in your darkest moments remember you are a grand Red Oak. Today I give you the name "Rooty Eike". "Rooty" means "red, root and light". So when you feel like all is dark, say your name, take root and you will find the light. "Eike" means "oak" or "tree". It also means "to blow and sing". So let your light shine and sing to inspire your inner self. When you feel like giving up, just whisper your name. You, my son, are a majestic Red Oak.' Rooty's mother was very sad. She knew Rooty would soon feel all alone. All she could do now was hope, pray and believe.

"As little Rooty looked up at his mother and thanked her for his name, he heard footsteps coming closer and closer to him: crunch, crunch, crunch. He closed his eyes tight and hoped the sound would pass him by. 'Oh, Mother,' he cried, 'What is that sound? I am scared.'

"'Remember your name, Rooty,' his mother called.

"Crunch crunch crunch. Again he heard the sound getting closer and closer until the ground trembled beneath him. 'Oh, please go away,' he thought in his heart. All of a sudden the sound stopped right next to Rooty.

Then he felt a large, rough hand scoop him up. He opened his eyes and saw a man with curly hair and green eyes looking at him.

He saw the old man's lips move and thought that the man said, 'You will make a fine tree one day.' Rooty could not hear a sound, but he enjoyed the thought of being a fine tree.

"For a moment Rooty smiled, but then the old man put him into his deep pocket. Rooty's smile transformed into a sad cry. 'Oh, no, please don't take from my home! Please put me back! I am going to be a majestic Red Oak just li my mom some day. Please don't take me from my family. Help, help! Please someone help me! Mother, help me!'

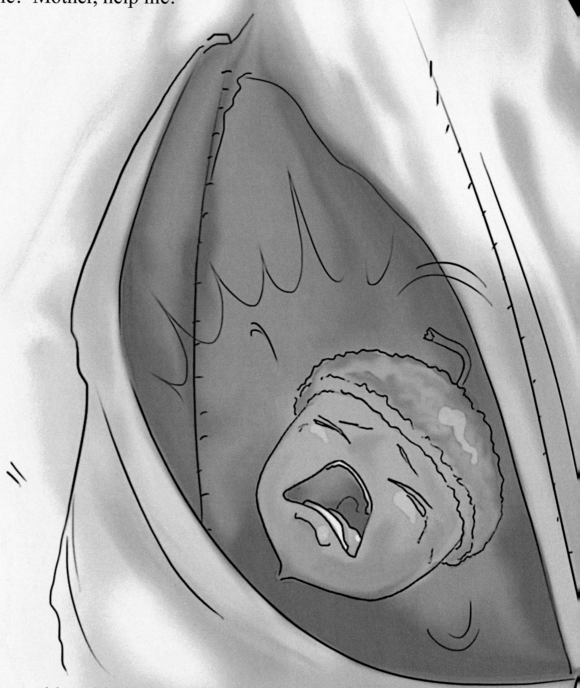

"But his mother could not help him any longer. 'Remember your name Rooty Eike, remember who you are and never lose hope. You are a majestic Red Oak.' His mother's voice faded as the old man walked away, and all Rooty could hear was *crunch crunch crunch* as he was tossed around in the darkness of the deep, dark pocket.

...not feeling well at all. He had been tossed up and down back and forth ...ss. He could not tell which way was up nor which way was down. ...man stopped and put his big, rough hand in his pocket and grabbed ... He lifted him up, up, up. Rooty opened his eyes, and once again he was ...ooking into the deep green eyes of the old man. Rooty's eyes filled with tears. The old man's eyes were the same color of the leaves on his mother's branches. Rooty tried to speak to the old man and begged again, 'Please bring me back to my forest! I want to grow up with my family and live with my mother. Please bring me home.'

The old man had gentle eyes and spoke kindly to the acorn, but Rooty could not hear him. Rooty watched the old man's lips, but this time it was too hard for him to understand any words. He was a little acorn, not a human like the old man. The acorn spoke in his heart, but the man spoke with his mouth. The man smiled at Rooty and said, "One day you shall be mighty and strong. I will watch over you and care for you. I have great plans for you, little one."

The old man held up a glass of water and said, "This will soften your shell and give you water that you will need in the days ahead. Soon the sun will be hot, and this will prepare you for that day."

But little Rooty could not hear nor understand the old man. He begged him
no, please! I don't live in water; I need the dirt; I live in the dirt! Please bring
home. Please don't put me in this water; I can't breathe. Help me, I will drown
here!"

The old man did not listen. He dropped Rooty in the water—*plop*—and walked
away. For three days the little acorn was in the water, and little by little he felt his
life slipping away. He remembered what his mother said. All he could do was
whisper his name, "Rooty, Rooty, Rooty Eike. I am a Red Oak, for my mother told
me so."

Rooty had no strength left, he fell asleep and thought he would die. ...came back and lifted him out of the water. Again the little acorn ...nose deep green eyes. 'It looks like you are ready,' said the old man. ...will be a fine tree some day.' But poor Rooty could not hear him. He could ...ot understand what the old man was saying.

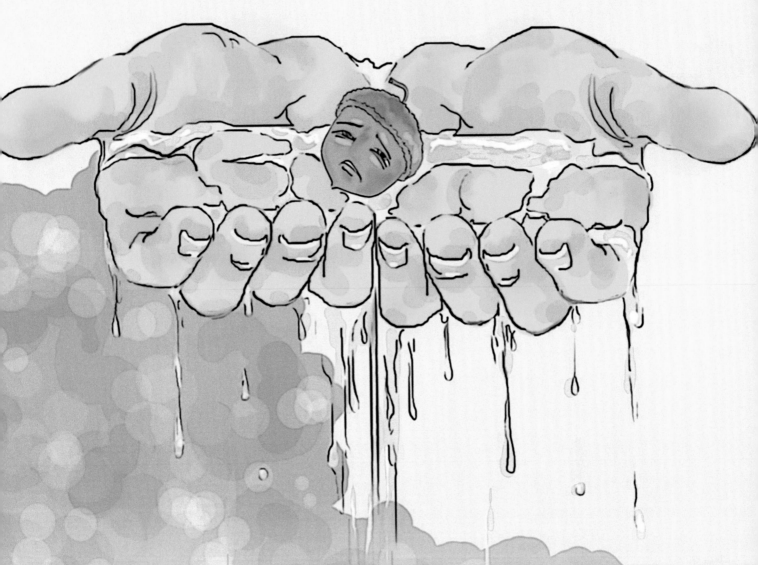

"The old man put the acorn back into his pocket, and again Rooty began to cry, 'Please, no, just bring me home! Please take me to my mother. I am a Red Oak and I belong in the majestic forest. Please put me back in the dirt.'

"As the old man walked, Rooty was tossed around, up, down, back and forth in the deep, dark pocket. All Rooty could do was remember his mother's words: 'Whisper your name and never lose hope. You must believe and remember that you are a majestic Red Oak. You are roots and light, you are inspiration and song.'

"Little Rooty closed his eyes and whispered his name over and over, 'Rooty, Rooty Eike.' Just then he felt the familiar rough hand lift him out of the pocke again. But this time the old man lifted him up and looked at him with those de green eyes and said, 'You are ready. Today your transformation begins. You shall be a mighty Red Oak.'

"Again the little acorn could not understand. He did not speak with lips like a man. With all his might, deep in his heart he begged and prayed the old man to put him back in the dirt next to his mother.

n, the little acorn felt the old man put him in soft, cool dirt. 'Oh, yes,' home. I am back in the soft dirt.' Then Rooty opened his eyes only e was not home, but was in a pot filled with dirt. His little heart sank. t he was not in the water and he was not in the deep, dark pocket. He loved e dirt and it made him feel a little closer to home. As he was looking around, he saw many pots filled with dirt and lots of acorns just like him everywhere. What was this place? How horrible for all of these little acorns to be out of the forest in these lonely little pots.

"Then he saw that big, rough hand coming towards him again. Down, down, down, straight for him, but this time it did not pick him up nor put him in the deep, dark pocket. This time it picked up some dirt and put the dirt right on top of Rooty. Rooty began to yell, 'No, no, please, I don't like the dark! Please don't cover me in dirt. I am meant to see the sky, to feel the rain and the wind. Stop; please let me out!' But the old man again did not listen. He picked up the pot, moved it into the sun, and poured water into the dirt that covered the little acorn.'

"All alone and in the dark, Rooty heard the words of his mother, 'Just whisper your name and don't lose hope. Remember you are Rooty Eike, roots, light, inspiration and song. You are a majestic Red Oak.'

"Rooty began to cry and whisper his name. He did not feel hope; he just said his name to help him remember his mother's voice. He missed her so much, and all he wanted was to see her again. Rooty found it hard to believe that would ever happen. All he had left of her was the name she gave him on the day he fell in that terrible, mean storm. 'Rooty, Rooty, Rooty Eike,' he whispered, until he fell asleep.

"He began to dream of the wind—swish swish—and the rain—drip drop, drip drop. He imagined a beautiful blue sky. Drip drop, swish swish. Drip drop swish swish. As he was dreaming, the sun began to warm the dirt where he lay. It got hotter and hotter and hotter. When Rooty woke up his stomach ached and his chest hurt. He was swelling up and felt like he would explode. He got hotter and hotter, and could not take the heat any longer.

"All of a sudden, Rooty heard crack, creek, pop! He yelled in pain. Then his shell broke and he felt a great relief. He called, 'I'm free; I'm free!" Something was different, he realized, as he began to grow and move and stretch farther and farther. But something was also wrong. He was not going up; he was going down, down, down, to the right and to the left. He was a tree; trees grow up not down.

"Rooty was afraid and did not know what to do. In desperation, he began to say his name, but this time it was not a whisper. 'Rooty, Rooty, Rooty Eike! Rooty, Rooty, Rooty Eike!' He gave one last giant push and yelled, 'Rooty Eike!' as the earth above him broke. He saw the light. He cried, 'I am a tree, a majestic Red Oak, and my name is Rooty Eike!'

"Rooty opened his eyes and saw that he was free, but he no longer was an acorn. He had leaves like his mother and he had roots, a stem and a base. He was a sapling, a little baby tree. He looked around and saw others who looked just like him. All the pots around him were filled with little saplings. It looked like a little baby forest. Just then he saw that familiar big, rough hand. Rooty's heart skipped a beat as the hand lifted him up, up, up. He saw those deep green eyes again. 'There you are, little one. I have been waiting for you.'

"A miracle had happened. Even though the old man spoke with his lips, Rooty could hear him this time. 'I can hear you,' said Rooty to the old man. 'Yes, I know,' replied the old man. 'You have grown out of your acorn shell. It was hard, and it prevented you from hearing me. It was given to you for your protection as you had to endure all of those hard times. Now you are free from that shell and you have grown to see the light. You never lost hope; you endured the darkness and believed that you were created to be a majestic Red Oak. You never let go of your faith. Now you shall see all that you dreamed of come to pass. You shall be planted by a river and you shall bring shade and shelter. Your branches shall be home to many animals that need you. You will be a safe haven and a place of peace.'

'Rooty, you can call me Paw Paw if you like. I love trees and forests of all kinds. You may not remember, but when you were very small, still hanging on the branch of your mother, a great wind brought a lot of destruction and a forest was destroyed. I gathered you and all of the others you see around you. I have watched over you and cared for you and I have believed in you. I waited until you were ready. Now the day has come and you are ready to be planted by the river. Can you trust me, and are you willing to go to a new place and be part of this grand new forest?'

'Oh, yes, Paw Paw!' Rooty exclaimed. 'I am sorry I did not trust you before; I could not hear you and I did not understand your heart. But now that I know you and all that you have done, I am willing to go with you anywhere you desire. I love you, Paw Paw.'

'You are well rooted and you are filled with light, Rooty. Just like the name your mother gave you, Rooty Eike. You are an inspiration, for you never gave up. Well done, little one. I love you too.'

'Thank you, Paw Paw,' Rooty whispered."

Paw Paw looked at the faces of his little grandchildren as he was telling the story, and he paused for a little while just to see them smile.

One of the grandchildren asked "Paw Paw, what happened to Rooty? Can we go see him in the great forest?"

"Why, of course you can! Close your eyes, lift your head to the sky and then look up."

All of the children did as Paw Paw said. They closed their eyes, lifted their heads and then looked up.

Paw Paw then said, "Do you see this grand tree that you are sitting under?"

They all said in unison, "Yes!"

Then the wind began to gently blow, and Paw Paw said, "This, my children, is Rooty Eike. You are sitting in his cool shade."

Rooty caught the wind with his leaves and gently carried it down to the ground, tickling all of the children and Paw Paw on their cheeks. They all said, "Ahhhh!" and giggled.

The littlest grandchild then raised her hand and asked, "Paw Paw, did Rooty ever see his mother again?"

"Oh, my, what a great question. You better believe it. Look over there," said Paw Paw as he pointed across the river. "You see the biggest tree in the forest? Well, that is Olivia, and that is Rooty's mom."

The wind blew and blew, and Olivia waved her branches at all of the children. They waved back. Everyone clapped and said, "Yea, Rooty! Yea, Olivia!"

The littlest grand child got up and ran to her Paw Paw and hugged his neck.
"Thank you, Paw Paw."

"For what, little one?"

"For Rooty, Paw Paw. For Rooty."

POSTSCRIPT

To all the children and children at heart: Thank you for reading the story of Rooty Eike. I hope you love this little acorn as much as my granddaughters, Anna and Molly, do. Here at our home we have lots of little acorns growing into grand oaks. Just like Rooty, we all must endure the trials of life and overcome obstacles in order to become all that we were created to be. I pray that this book will bring you courage in the place of fear and hope in the place of despair each and every time you read it, so that you never give up and are able to achieve all of your dreams too.

Angela and Michael Bertone Sr.

ABOUT THE AUTHOR

Angela Q. Bertone was born and raised in Livingston, Louisiana, and is one of six children. She gives honor to her mother, and credits her with passing down the art of storytelling. She finds joy in remembering her mother's gift for crafting her own original stories, as well as for bringing the tales of others to life by providing each character with a unique voice. One of Angela's childhood favorites is the tale of Br'er Fox and Br'er Rabbit, from a full-color, illustrated hardback version of Joel Chandler Harris's Uncle Remus.

Angela followed in her mother's footsteps and often performed "dinner theater" with her children. She dressed herself and her children as different story characters while they shared lunch and watched movies. She even spoke in character as she served her children, hoping to pass on her mother's traditions and her enthusiasm for storytelling.

Today, Angela is fulfilling her dream of becoming a published author with multiple releases and is now the creator and host of "Dishing It Out--Louisiana Style", a national cooking show.

Her first book is a self-published spiritual/inspirational work called *Good Mourning Sunshine*. Read more about Angela and her writing on her website, www.angelabertone.com

ABOUT THE ILLUSTRATOR

This book was illustrated and designed by Louisiana native, Ariane O'Pry Trammell. Art is her passion and fulltime occupation. She works within a broad spectrum of styles and mediums. This allows her to create ideal custom pieces to meet the specific needs of her clients and to produce one of a kind works of art such as portraits, murals, sculptures, book illustrations, paintings, drawings, graphic design and caricatures. She specializes in book layout and design, assisting clients throughout the self-publishing process. Ariane is also an author, having released her first children's book, *Where the Grass is Always Greener*, in the spring of 2014. Please visit her website at *www.arianesart.com* to see more of her work and stay up to date on future projects.

69118291R00020

Made in the USA
San Bernardino, CA
12 February 2018